COYOTE

Colin Winnette

Coyote
FIRST EDITION

Text and cover design by Les Figues Press

ISBN 13: 978-1-934254-56-1
ISBN 10: 1-934254-56-8
Library of Congress Control Number: 2014947072

Les Figues Press thanks its subscribers for their support and readership.
Les Figues Press is a 501c3 organization. Donations are tax-deductible.

Les Figues thanks the following individuals for their generosity:
Peter Binkow and Johanna Blakley, Lauren Bon, Elena Karina Byrne, Nicholas Karavatos,
Coco Owen, and Dr. Robert Wessels.

Les Figues Press titles are available through:
Les Figues Press, http://www.lesfigues.com
Small Press Distribution, http://www.spdbooks.org

Thank you to each of the following individuals for assisting with the NOS contest: Aimee
Bender, Melissa Buzzeo, Teresa Carmody, Michael du Plessis, Veronica Gonzalez-Peña, Doug
Nufer, Coco Owen, and Andrew Wessels. In producing this book, special thanks to Les Figues
interns: Fisayo Adeyeye, Amber Donofrio, Allie Maher, Sara Newman, Becky Robison,
Crystal Salas, and Genevieve Shifke.

Post Office Box 7736
Los Angeles, CA 90007
info@lesfigues.com
www.lesfigues.com

For any always elsewhere.

COYOTE

WE WERE ON the porch most of the night before she vanished. Just grilling and eating things like hot dogs and potatoes. Her Dad grilled the buns so they got all sweet and burnt-tasting on the edges. We drank beers and watched her pick at the heads of nails sticking up out of the splintering blue wood. Her Dad played guitar a little, songs I didn't know other than when he played them.

I didn't like to drink in front of her. I never got comfortable with it, not really. But that night I just gave into it and drank and she seemed happy enough and even her Dad seemed a little happy. Or at least that's how I remember it.

It was getting dark but we sat out a little longer while the bugs gathered up to the house lights. They were in her long hair, getting tangled. She got a bite or something that made her come over and get up in my lap. Coyotes used to come by all the time back then, but I can't remember if they did that night or not. We'd hear them circling and sounding off like maniacs, real high-pitched wailing like some hysterical woman lost out in the woods.

One time one came right up onto the porch and her Dad got him with a shovel while I watched from the kitchen. He cracked it once and then a few more times for good measure. He wanted to eat the thing, brought it inside wrapped in a t-shirt from the thrift bag, but there was no way she or I was going to get involved with that. So he buried it in the yard with the dog, two cats, and a hamster from before. The roads near us aren't busy, but they're busy enough. They're constantly littered with all kinds of dead or dying. Everything that escapes winds up out there eventually. That's the way it seems at least. Her Dad has brought every escapee back to us in a tarp.

I'VE TOLD THE SAME story over and over again, to the police, to the reporters, to the prep-interviewers and interviewers and celebrity guests and you name it. I tell the same story every time: we put her to bed, and when we woke up she was gone.

THE FIRST TIME I thought being a mother might have deranged me, I was watching her play in the yard. This was back when Spot was alive, our first dog. All black with a white spot on his chest. Creative people, we aren't really. She was throwing sticks and he was chasing them. I only went inside for a second, to fill my glass, but I heard Spot cry out and then he was there at the back porch. I couldn't tell where the blood was coming from at first. It hid in streams of long black hair, pooling in the white diamond at his chest, dyeing the whole thing red as a new car.

Before I brought him in I scanned the yard for her, but I didn't see her so I went looking. Spot stayed on the porch, whimpering a little and wanting some help, I'm sure, but I was getting a little worried, wondering where she might have gone to. Your mind starts filling with so many ideas about what could have happened.

I pictured someone cutting her and Spot, someone hurting them, someone taking her, running away with her. I even pictured her as a monster, just a little bit. Not that I didn't forgive her immediately. She wouldn't have known what she was doing. I'd done things as a kid that were hurtful, dangerous, just not knowing. I killed a few animals through sheer curiosity and aggressive ignorance. Drowned a hamster, suffocated a cat beneath a mattress. I never meant any harm.

I pictured her experimenting with Spot. The ways she might have hurt him without understanding the cruelty of what she'd done. And it was right when those images were at the peak of intensity that I found her in the bushes, just crying and curled up there, innocent as Eve.

Spot started hurting, she told me later.

I had carried her into the house, crying there in my arms, and set her on the counter by the sink. I wiped at her face with a rag but every tear I wiped away was immediately replaced with a new one.

How did he start hurting?

He just did, she said. She was open-mouthed crying then, like a wail, like she did when she was a baby.

So I let it drop.

I didn't care what happened anymore. I just wanted her to stop crying. I held her as close to my heart as possible. I don't know why, but I get the feeling it's warmest there. She balled up in my arms and I held her while she cried and I bounced her. I swayed a little, watched the window. It was just a normal afternoon, with that sharp afternoon light on the curtains. I watched that until she seemed weightless in my arms. Until she grew quiet and her sounds were replaced by Spot's there at the door. It could have been a human being, begging, and it wouldn't have mattered to me. I only wanted her to quiet down and curl up.

HER DAD AND I don't sleep anymore, but we still get into bed. We shut our eyes from time to time, until our eyelids get sore or just seem to open up on their own. We'll be quiet for hours. Not tossing, not turning. Just there on our backs with our arms at our sides or folded in our laps. I ask him, What was our daughter like?, and he can only say one hundred percent true things that can't be argued.

She was without visible flaws, he says.

She had tiny hands, like a puppy that is never going to get any bigger.

She had thin brown hair.

She ate what we worried might be too much ketchup, liked it on tacos.

She preferred her water warm.

She wasn't scared of anything, even the coyotes.

She really only cried when she could tell we thought she might. She was an opportunist.

She reminded me of the scarred-up girls in high school. Quiet, funny, solitary, like the best thing I could do for her was to stay out of her way.

She worried about the characters in books from the very first page. Is he sad? she would ask. Over and over.

ALL OF HER TOYS were put away. The bed was made, as if we'd never placed her in it. The back door was open, but the screen was closed. That's the way we did it during the fall. The way we'd done it for years. The screen door slams, and we've been meaning to fix it. It's loud enough for us to notice. But neither of us did. If she went out, if someone came in, we should have heard it. But we didn't hear anything.

Her Dad and I fought the next night. He took it upon himself to burn all the pictures. What got into him? Beer, I guess. Something strong, maybe. He spends nearly all his home time in a folding chair on the porch or on his back in bed. He was there and I came out and said, Where are all the pictures?

After a moment, he told me he'd burned them. Dug a hole in the yard and burned them and most of the toys and kid diapers and a bunch of things he couldn't remember. Then he buried it all.

I screamed at him, of course, and demanded to know what right he thought he had and that kind of thing, and he took it for a while until he decided he couldn't do that anymore and we started hitting one another. Hitting is one of those things everyone tells themselves they would never put up with. Then you get shoved one night during a fight that's more intense than usual. If you're me, and you've got a two year-old who's looking up to you, you shove back. If you're lucky, it ends there and you skulk around feeling mad for days and swearing you're going to leave if he ever does something like that again. And he doesn't, not for months. Then there's another shove, maybe a push, a hand raised, something like that. And it's the same thing all over again, only you get over it a little more easily. You drive your daughter around, talking to her all the while. You drive and watch the road and ask questions, as if to an empty car. Then a little voice somewhere in the back chirps up, says something about fences and cows, sounding so in love with the world that you just forget most of what's horrible and feel grateful for what you have. However little it is. You head home and find him there and he's different. You hold onto the shove like a photograph of a dead relative. Every now and then, when you look at it, you feel something stirring. But mostly your thoughts turn elsewhere.

MY THOUGHTS ARE ALWAYS turning elsewhere. I look at one thing for a bit, then I turn to another in mid-thought. Her Dad calls it "fluttering." It's why I'm a lousy cook. It's why the house is filled with little piles. A few magazines here, some mail with return services requested. Her Dad used to get sad a lot about nothing. It felt like a similar thing. We would be sitting out back or riding in the car, having a perfectly nice time, or a quiet time, at least, and he would just take on this look of intense sadness. It was always "nothing." His thoughts had just turned.

But when you have a child, that kind of thing doesn't fly. It's when you're not paying attention that they suddenly seem to need it most. When we were alone, her Dad and me, our minds could wander. He could dig deep into whatever sadness he was feeling and drink it out or just stare until his eyes began to water. And I could flutter. But with her around, it was different. She snapped us into focus. That's not to say we didn't drift. We just couldn't get lost anymore.

I CUT OFF her Dad's hair one night. Cut my own too. I can't say exactly when it was. He used to have this long hair, tied up in a ponytail most of the time. It came off with a couple snips, in one big clump. It was wild to look at, gathered up in a little black tie. He was asleep in a chair on the porch. He didn't even wake up. But he came in when I was working at mine. Hunched over the sink, just cutting whatever felt right. He didn't even know all that I'd done. He only asked me why I was doing what I was doing. And I didn't have an answer. So he watched for a little while then went to bed. And then he noticed.

I STILL DON'T KNOW why I did the hair thing. It was otherwise a pretty good day. A hollowed-out branch the length of our house broke loose from an oak in the backyard the day before. Her Dad went at it with a chainsaw, chopping it down to small blocks for firewood and for selling. It was dead wood mostly, not particularly useful. But he kept at it for hours, and I just watched from the porch. Some days I can sit back and do nothing at all, and this was one of those days. I was a nurse for awhile, but I'm not anymore. At least I don't think I am. I stopped going and no one's said anything to me about it. Maybe if I showed up in my scrubs, clocked in, and went about my day, no one would say anything about that either. Maybe I'll try it some day.

He took a shower after piling the wood and sat with me on the porch. He fell asleep there after only a few minutes, one of those little naps he used to take without warning. I watched him for a while then started to feel anxious. I can't say what about. I would if I could, but I just don't remember exactly. It had something to do with the way he was breathing. It seemed insufficient, like maybe he wasn't getting enough air. I saw it as a joke, my coming at him with the scissors. I kept imagining that he would wake up right as I was about to do it and I thought it would be funnier and funnier the closer I was to finishing the cut. Then I finished the cut. There was nothing really that funny about it. So I set at my own, to see if that could work too. The joke didn't land. It just made me feel crazy. We fought a little but he gave up pretty quick. After that, neither of us could get to sleep. That might have been the first time.

It's six months exactly since we were last on a talk show. The host was this sad guy, someone we'd never heard of, but we'd started doing the shows so we had to keep doing them. If we turned one down, we weren't looking as hard as we could. We were doing less than before, which meant she was dying in our minds, if not already dead.

The first show we went on was the big one. The Jerry Summers Show. It's not like the others at all. Not exploitative, sensational, those things. It's a wholesome show. We used to watch it when she was little, and Jerry would tell us tips and tricks on how to keep her healthy and happy, how to keep the house healthy and happy. Tips like things to spice up the lunchbox—mix salsa in with the sour cream, put it on a turkey sandwich. Leans out the sour cream, adds a little spicy kick, as well as a few diced vegetables. Anyway, I'm not ashamed to say I was a little excited to meet Jerry Summers. Most people would say they didn't care, that they were only thinking of their daughter. I didn't think any less of her—she hasn't left my mind since the day she arrived—but I made extra room for Jerry. He was in there with her, in my mind, telling her it was going to be okay. Telling us both.

And then he was telling us in person. Her Dad hired this woman to screen the phone calls, the interview questions, that kind of thing. He gave her a list of things we didn't want to talk about. Things that might trigger a bad reaction, render us speechless or distraught. We

were going to be on TV. We needed to be clear and direct and hold
it together. Those were the three things we said to one another as
we drove to the lot where they film the Jerry Summers Show. Then
Jerry was telling us it would be okay. He put his hands on me. Jerry
Summers touched my shoulders, my face. He held me. He told me
everything was going to be okay, that he would help us find her, help
with anything we needed. We had a dressing room with a fruit basket.
We had a make-up man. A little gay fellow who was so sweet when
he explained that I wouldn't be wearing much make-up, he wouldn't
be doing much to my hair. It was important that I look as upset as I
felt, but not like a complete wreck. It was a fine balance, he told me.
Everyone at the Jerry Summers Show was optimistic. It was a good
place to be. I was scared and hopeful. I ate candy after candy from a
dish on the shelf in front of the make-up man's mirror. His name was
Sonny, the make-up man. And that's exactly what he was.

I hardly remember the Jerry Show at this point. I don't have a
memory at all anymore. It was bright as hell and there was an audience
out there somewhere making sounds whenever I spoke and even more
sounds whenever Jerry spoke. I pictured a chorus of animals in the
seats, bellowing. Jerry kept talking about a number at the bottom of
the screen. Call this number, call this number. He asked me if I wanted
to say anything to the kidnappers, or whoever might have her, and I
had so many things I wanted to say. But the make-up man had told me
the one thing to say. The simplest, most effective thing. Please return
our daughter.

When we got in the car, her Dad told me I had been clear, direct,
and that I held it together. That was a day I did it right.

But the last one wasn't like that. After Jerry, I lost track. The woman
her Dad got to field the phone calls and the interview questions started

calling us all the time. Everyone wanted us to talk on their talk show, and everyone wanted us to say the same thing. Please return our daughter. We were celebrities and all. It was great stuff.

But the last guy just kind of slumped around on stage like an elephant. There was no audience, just a room with two cameras and some boys with microphones. It's all hazy at this point, but her Dad got tired of answering and told the host so. The host kept on, so eventually her Dad stood up, unclipped his little mic, and stormed off the set.

I sat there. All eyes on me. Few people know pressure like that. Talking to the entire world as if they were your daughter's kidnappers, murderers, adopters, whatevers. The host asked me how things were at home, how we were doing after all of this, nearly a year now. I wanted to tell him we were all right, not sleeping much, we had our disagreements and our dark times, but we were actually much calmer overall now, just waiting for our daughter to appear again, just waiting for anything, really. But my mind started to wander a little.

I told him about how she used to push her friends around. She was the bossiest little brat on the block. Kids would come over and she'd put them to work making mud pies, cleaning sticks out of the yard, adding vines—simple, curving lines were all she would allow—to some kind of mural of sidewalk drawings in pastel chalks.

They could tell I was proud. They could tell how much I loved her. It was a good little anecdote, and it came out of left field. I was funny, proud, sad, charming, spontaneous, the whole bit. I told jokes I can't remember. I never remember how I've charmed a person, only that I've done it. It never does me any good again, what they call an "on" night. I'm just grateful for them when they come, because things are momentarily easy. Even kind of nice. That's all I remember. A brief sense of relief. The rest washes away.

I floored them that night, and then I lost it. I was not clear or direct, and I did not hold it together. And everyone was moved. Even the host. I could feel the whole world sigh at once. I broke and that sigh became a gasp. I just wept there in my chair until the credits began to roll. Next thing I knew I was sitting in my chair at home, the red chair by the window where I sit and wait sometimes, or just sit and stare sometimes, and I was crying and sobbing and her Dad was there with a coffee or a tea or something else steaming, but I didn't look at it. I just kept losing it late into the night when he had already gathered himself up in bed and turned out the light to stare at the darkness. I finally traced his steps into the bedroom and got in next to him, still in my clothes and make-up, and we just stared into a lightless room together, not hearing any of the sounds outside, only the hearts in our chests thumping away all dull and regular like everything else.

WHAT WAS OUR daughter like?

She was like you today on that show.

She stuck out a bee sting one time. Came in out of the backyard with the stinger poking out of her arm, without shedding a tear.

She called herself Delilah.

She buttered her toast with her finger, no matter how many times we told her not to.

Punishments did not deter her from doing again what had brought about the punishment.

She laughed a lot. Most often to herself. She often refused to tell what it was she was laughing at.

She always left food on her plate because she claimed to like the feeling of scraping it into the trashcan with her fork.

AFTER THAT, the shows stopped calling. Or her Dad told the woman to stop letting them through, or to only let the good ones through, and the good ones never called. I can't say what happened other than our phone stopped ringing. After a few months, I went and cut the cord with a pair of safety scissors, so I could stop worrying about it. Stop expecting it to ring. It was a smooth snip, like running a spoon through butter.

Nearly a week went by before her Dad noticed what I'd done. He might never have noticed, but we had a storm and the house saw the worst of it. A branch came through a window in the living room. Bees came swarming out from beneath the stairs, he told me. Something must have broken loose under the house. They came flooding out in a little black cloud. Loud enough to be heard over the rain, the thunder, and the sound of her Dad running around the house doing God knows what. I was in the bathtub and a little bee came and sat on the mirror over the sink. I didn't notice it at first, didn't think anything of it when I finally did. Just a little crack in the glass, a streak or something. And when it moved, I figured it was a fly. Then more came and I started hearing the unmistakable hum of insects moving in a large group. I submerged myself in bath water up to my ears. I watched them swim around in the steam up above my head. I heard her Dad cursing about something. A bee landed on the curving top part of my ear and I swear

I could hear it rubbing together its hairy little legs. I knew not to budge though. Even when a few more gathered on the wet threads of my hair. I watched them and I thought about whatever and I waited.

When the rain finally stopped, most of the bees were still in there with me. Her Dad was out checking the lights, the cable, the phone line. Nothing was working. Nothing was as it should be.

I slowly dunked my head, and the bees lifted. I rose out of the water, lifted myself out of the tub, and exited the bathroom, as if in one swift motion. Her Dad was in the living room, sweeping up glass and laughing.

The bathroom's full of bees, I told him.

He held out his hand, all swollen and dotted with red bumps. He told me he knew.

He said I looked good like that and I remembered then that I was naked. When I started toward the bedroom, he told me that the bees came from there, from the stairs I was headed toward. He gave me a jacket from the closet by the back door, and I listened to him sweep up the glass and branches. I watched as he put a magazine or two back on the coffee table. He was going to tape the window, he said. And call the electrician. And the cable guy. And the phone company.

Sometimes, I push my cuticles back with the nails on the opposite hand. It looks like I'm picking at the ends of my nails. It looks like I'm nervous, so he always asks. It's happened so often for so long, I don't feel like I have to say anything in response anymore.

HER DAD ISN'T STRONG. That's why he's always doing things around the house. He's little, really. So he chops up trees, fixes the chairs, replaces the light bulbs, climbs on this and bends that back into shape. He's always been thin, but he's thinner now. Thinner than he's ever been. Me too, I guess.

He wants to fill a room. He wants to be a presence. He doesn't say it, but he's the kind of prey that tries to look like some other animal. He's a little fox or something, standing on its hind legs, baring its teeth.

The point is, we're pretty much evenly matched when we go at it. It's anybody's fight. So sometimes I just let him wail on me. I let him feel strong. It's not something I'm proud of. I let some punches get through. I let him pin me. I put up my hands, as if to fight him back. But sometimes there's no fight in me. Only love. How strange does that sound? That you could love someone who's hitting you? I don't hate myself. It's more than that. I wouldn't know how to say it. I can tell some part of him is proud, but an even bigger part is hating himself for what he's done. And that's worse than me hating him, the way he hates himself. And I like that, too.

THIS ONE TIME, I hit him with a lamp. It wasn't a hard hit but it toppled him. He came up completely out of fight. His hand was at his mouth. He looked sad and young and scared and there was blood on his fingertip. It wasn't anything serious. I'd hit his mouth, pushed some teeth through his upper lip, chipped the end of one.

I got him an ice pack and he said he was sorry for whatever it was that had started us fighting. That's exactly what he said, Whatever it was.

The next morning I got out of bed before him. I brought my open mouth down on the edge of the counter top. I didn't manage to chip the exact same tooth, but I chipped one that was near enough to it. I fainted or passed out or something and woke up on the porch, where he had propped me up. Not like a rag doll, but like something you want to rest awhile. Like maybe he set her down sometimes. A tender kind of propping.

WHAT WAS OUR daughter like?

If given the choice, she would not eat hard things. Anything that was stiff. Anything that crunched. Given the choice, she would always choose soft things.

She pet the cat against its fur, in spite of the fact that I told her many times that it was the wrong way.

Even before she could speak, she looked at us like she was listening. Her eyes followed the sound passing back and forth between us or pointed directly at her.

THIS HANDSOME DETECTIVE used to come by the house, but always at the wrong time. He called himself Mc-something. He was an Irish cop with a drinking problem, just like on the TV shows. I know it because he looked tired and sort of weak in the knees. He always accepted water when I offered. His thirst was unquenchable.

He always came when her Dad was out, so we couldn't both give him a statement. I told him the story I told everyone: we put her to bed, and when we woke up, she was gone. That's the whole of the story. No, nobody had any reason to want to do us or her harm. No, we didn't have any money or receive any requests for money or strange phone calls. The only people who called wanted to interview us. They were just like us. They just wanted to know more.

He took notes. He had a round belly, bigger than his arms and face would suggest, and he set the pad on his belly sometimes when he was sitting in a chair on the porch or in the living room. He wasn't unfriendly, but he wasn't someone I would talk to normally. He was just doing his job, I guess. He seemed to care. He seemed to take it personally. I don't know why I felt that way, but it was the way I felt. He said her name over and over again, as if he were trying to memorize it, but he never hesitated, never struggled to remember. It seemed an unnecessary measure taken out of respect and fear.

I like his type of cop. It's a different type than the cops I've met in our neighborhood, the cops who came when someone shot BBs through the front window, or the cops who came when there was a car parked at the end of our street for days, or the cops who write speeding tickets where the limit drops as Oak Street becomes East Oak Street. Those cops aren't like you'd expect. They're just these nice-ish guys, kind of dumb, but not too dumb, just filling out these forms and nodding and smiling and uninterested. They might as well be bank tellers. They're not invested. Mc-something seemed invested. He was a special kind of cop, maybe.

WHEN I FIRST told her Dad about Mc-something, he asked questions like, Did you see his badge? Did he have a warrant to come in? Did he tell you what they were doing, how they were looking? How do cops look for someone? Do they patrol with lights at nighttime? Go door-to-door? Do they dig up yards? Drain lakes? What's the protocol? What's the plan? What's their angle? What's his take?

I said he's trying to help so why bother about it. He's not hurting anything. There was no reason to get worked up. I told him, I think they dig up all the yards and fill them back in. I think they swim around in lakes in scuba gear and shine lights on old ships and secret fish. I think they find more than they're looking for, but never what they're looking for. I think he's a special kind of cop with a chip on his shoulder. He seems like he needs something in his life. I don't know if he's married or not, but he doesn't act like a married man. He seems confused and unsure what to do with his body. If he's got a wife, she's unhelpful. I think he's the kind of cop who will track this thing down to the bitter end. I think he's the kind of cop who takes it personally. He's the kind who would turn in his badge, but keep hold of his gun.

Mc-something?

Yeah, Mc-something. Or just Mick. He's Irish.

I get it, he said. Mick Something.

Mick Something Goes Rogue.

Mick Something Goes Wild.

We fuck all of the time now, me and her Dad. We've got more time on our hands than we know what to do with. It's not great fucking. It's pretty casual most of the time. Sometimes it gets intense. Typically more so for one of us than the other. I'll get this rush of some feeling and just start fucking him like I'm wringing a cat's neck. I get on top and he grips my hips or the sides of my legs and I just set to work on him, tilting myself to get the right angle, so it's like he's one of those alien babies in that movie *Aliens*, breaking out of my stomach. It doesn't feel like that, but that's what I picture when I'm trying to get the angle right. Right before he's about to come, he always looks shocked, as if it never occurred to him that it would happen. When I come, I think I look mean. That's just what I guess. I always feel like I'm taking something from him. Taking something for myself. Absorbing his energy or something. He likes it, but he gets pale sometimes, like I'm making a face he couldn't otherwise stand to see. Or that used to be true. He's getting used to it now, I think. He looks away sometimes, closes his eyes. I resent orgasms most of the time because I don't like the "finishing up" feeling that comes after. I'd rather just keep going. But I also hate tiring out, wearing down, which always happens eventually, if we're not smart enough to chase an orgasm for ourselves whenever one's in sight.

Yesterday, I was pretty sure I saw Mick driving past the house. I didn't recognize the car—it was a brown something—but the guy in the driver's seat had this simmering determination all about him. He drove slow, watching the road and searching for something in the passenger seat with his right hand. I could see that much from the porch. He didn't look over at me. Mick Something playing it cool. Trying to play it like he wasn't checking in on us, like he didn't want to make sure we were getting along, living our lives, still waiting for him to return our daughter.

I told her Dad.

I'm pretty sure I saw Mc-something.

Her Dad was on his back, beneath the sink.

Is it broken?

Tightening up, said her Dad. So it doesn't become broken.

Tightening what?

These... things.

He pulled himself out from under the sink, pointed with his toe toward a dark area.

He was trying to play it cool, I said. Reaching over like he was getting at something in the passenger's seat. So cool I didn't even catch his glance. But he was looking.

Mick Something?

Yeah.

Leaning over him, I could see him swelling against his jeans.

You fucking love Mick, I said.

He had a whole list of things to do, her Dad did. He showed me the list. The sink was at the top. So I let him by.

What was she like?

She spoke out of order. I assumed it was because she got overexcited. For example, she might have just said: She ordered out of spoke. She laughed at herself when she did it. I suspected she might have made some mistakes on purpose.

She did not tolerate silence. She filled the days and evenings with sound.

She sang often, songs we did not teach her. Songs she must have come up with herself, or picked up at school.

She called me Dad, Dada, Dod, and Daddy. I tried to get her to call me Pop, but she did not pick it up.

She was stubborn.

WE GOT THE CABLE fixed and Jerry Summers had someone on who'd killed somebody without knowing it. There's a sleep thing where you do what you're dreaming, but in real life. This guy just woke up with his dead wife's neck in his hands. Jerry was sweet to the guy, who was positioned in a chair between two policemen, his hands chained together. Jerry asked him what it felt like, what he had to say to the world, to his wife's family, to himself, and the guy said, I did an unforgivable thing. Jail's the very least of my punishment. I'm going to live as good as I can until the day I die, because that's when the real punishment will start. Then the camera cut to Jerry, who was nodding, letting the microphone sag. Then the camera cut to the guy, who said, I am very truly sorry. He had just a little make-up on, mostly under the eyes. His hair was shining in the light because of the hairspray. Our make-up man was probably standing there, just off-camera, feeling proud as a child, happy as a clam. I don't think of him that often anymore. But I'm sure he's doing well. I remember he was that type of person.

THIS ONE TIME we cooked a whole boar on a spit in the backyard. This was before her. When her Dad was just him. He tried hunting for awhile, but was never very good at it. He liked being out in the woods with a gun. He liked drinking and sitting very very still. But he didn't like to shoot, he told me. Whenever he did spot something, a bird of some worthwhile kind or, once, a doe, it always seemed to come at a time when he was feeling particularly at peace with his silence. Comfortable and happy, he called it. So he wasn't ready to break that feeling with a shot, by taking a thing down. So he never once pulled the trigger in the right way.

He made friends, instead. He and his friends shot at cans and tree trunks. They went out for weekends and his friends loaded the beds of the trucks they drove with their kills. He never brought anything back. Except the one time with the boar.

According to him, it wasn't his kill. Something a friend donated at the end of a particularly successful day. He'd taken down a buck, a few pheasants, and two boars. More meat than he could eat. More than he really wanted to deal with. So the friend handed it over to him, free of charge. He'd bought the beer the night before, something along those lines.

I always doubted the truth of that story. That one of those boys would ever give up a clean kill, an entire boar. Wouldn't even take a picture of himself with it. These proud men. These men weighed their kills with a special kind of joy. They hung around gas stations and general stores, went out for breakfasts and talked for hours about what they'd been thinking, how they'd been feeling, how they had almost overlooked the beast, lingering there in the corner of their eye. How something hadn't felt right about the stillness, or whatever, so they looked a little more closely, they felt it in their gut, and the gut was hardly ever wrong.

That kind of man doesn't just hand over a boar like a handful of change. I've always suspected her Dad killed it himself. Finally decided to step up and be a man, and that he'd been lying to me all along. I think he wanted me to believe he was the kind of man who would never kill a thing. But I think the truth of the matter is that everyone is a killer, given the right order of things. Everyone has it in them.

He always had the fear in him that I might leave. Especially before she arrived. He knew he wasn't a great man, that he'd lucked out with me falling in love with him and all. It was one of those things that just happens, and you don't question it for years. But one day you start noticing the strangeness of it. That an ugly man, an abusive, stupid, weak, ugly man, could suddenly have someone at his side who loved him more than life.

First of all, I like an ugly man. I'm not ugly myself, but there's something vulnerable about an ugly man. He doesn't expect much from the world. He doesn't feel entitled. And, most often, ugly men know how to take care of themselves. They're used to being alone. It makes them self-sufficient. It breeds character. Also, hobbies. Ugly men take up all kinds of hobbies. They're good with their hands, or they've read more books than you'd care to think about. They can cook or fix things.

Her Dad tried for it all, which guaranteed he would never be particularly good at any of it, but it was cute to see him move about the house, tooling at one thing, flipping a few pages in the history of some ancient civilization that we might be better off forgetting, tying flies he'll never use, cleaning guns that will never be truly his because he never used them proper, and so on. I liked that kind of restlessness. It made sense to me. And I'll admit that some part of me thought I could calm him down enough to focus on a thing. It wasn't a thought I had, just a feeling. Or when I pictured us together, I pictured us calm and comfortable. I pictured my thoughts turning a little less and his hands working a little more steadily. I pictured us at a kind of peace I knew only from the picture in my head. I was wishing for us, I guess.

That kind of stillness didn't come until after she vanished. Before, we were too anxious and new to each other, and you're never still with a child around. Anybody knows that. But in some sense, afterwards, my wish came true. At least at night it did. We hardly move at night, except for when we're fucking. We mostly lie there and just be awake. For hours. I don't know how I could have ever wished for it, but I don't wish for it to go away. I don't wish for anything anymore, really. I just imagine her showing up again. I imagine her at the doorstep, over and over. But that image always gives way to the other places she could be. The other things that might be happening, or might have happened. I can't stop myself. So I don't wish for anything anymore.

THE BOAR.

He tied its feet together with twine from the garage. He brought out the poles we used to use for the volleyball net. They were some kind of solid metal held upright by concrete we'd poured into a couple of bald tires. He crossed them with another pole, left over from when he rebuilt the chain-link fence a few years back, and balanced it on two metal hooks sticking out of the vertical poles.

He shaved it on the back porch, washed it in the tub. When I peed later, there were flecks of boar shit splattered on the floor, the mirror, the tank. He cut a lead with his knife and rammed the fence pole through one end of the boar and out the other. It wasn't clean. It came out at an odd angle, leaving the boar's head to dangle a bit below the rest of him. Its little leathery nub of a tongue stuck out from between two grimacing lips, as if it were daring her Dad to light the fire.

He removed the head with a bread knife. The only saws we had were rusty and old, probably dull. He didn't want to spoil the neck meat. The sound was like rain on a carpet. It lasted a good fifteen minutes before he'd cut clean through. He brought the head into the house, carrying it by its ears. He set it in a pot, covered the pot, and brought a starter log with him when he came back out.

You'll burn it, I said.

He pulled a metal trashcan out from alongside the house, emptied the water inside onto the grass. Then he removed his shirt. He ran it along the inside of the can, trembling the corrugated metal with each swipe. He dropped the log into the dry can and followed it with a lit match. He stood over it until the flames took. They grew, and his beard and forehead began to shimmer orange and pink, like a sunset on silt.

I was watching his relationship to the kill, his hands on the corpse, how much he cared for it. His movements were quick, unceremonious. I began to believe he hadn't killed it. When he wasn't watching the fire, adding logs to the fire, he was considering the animal skewered on the fence pole between the vertical volleyball net supports. His expression was a mix of hunger and disgust.

Eventually the logs in the can turned to coal and ash and her Dad dumped the coals beneath the impaled boar. He turned it gingerly on the makeshift spit. He did so for hours, for the rest of the afternoon and into the night. He never flagged. He made batch after batch of coals in the can and turned the spit. I started to think he might have killed it, the way he tended to its turning.

I'm no detective. I'm no jittery but steadfast Mick Something. But I watched his face. Other times his hands. They seemed to say different things. The hands were unskilled, uncareful, uneasy. The face had a kind of brilliant focus to it. He was determined. It looked like hard work, and like he was up to the challenge. This might have been exactly what he wanted me to feel. He might have been leading me, and I might have followed wherever he wanted me to go.

WHAT WAS SHE LIKE?

She did not like any music but her own. She unplugged radios.

She only played with adult toys. She chose keys over a doll.

She snored a little bit in her sleep. You couldn't really hear it, but it was there.

THE MEAT HAD NOTHING good about it. Tough and flavorless, for the most part, but occasionally you'd get a moist piece. That was even worse. Grisly, fatty sludge. It came apart in your mouth like a hot marshmallow. I couldn't finish a plate, and he lost his temper.

He showed it by eating four plates himself. He told me a story while he ate, so I couldn't leave without interrupting him. Not without making a point of it.

His great-grandfather had overseen the building of a small bridge over a nasty creek. Intense rapids, deep water. Lots of mules and oxen lost, several families too. Gold Rush era families whose men were setting out to set them up for good. Their eyes glittered. They were determined in a way it is impossible to imagine, because there is nothing like it anymore. Her Dad's great-grandfather had both aided these men and taken a kind of advantage of them. He was an opportunist. He had a small crew from the town on the east side of the river, men who would soon be looking to get more easily past the creek themselves. It was an honest coming together. Every man needed something and each was willing to pull his own weight.

It was at this point that I decided he had not killed the boar. If he had killed the boar, the story would have been about the strength of the one man who spearheaded the endeavor. The hero who had brought everyone together and executed the perfect plan to make himself and the nation richer. But instead he kept going on about working together, one man lending one thing to another and everybody profiting in some unique and personal way.

These were a gutless man's dreams. That's not to say it was a cowardly vision. It was idealistic, something our truer selves might hope for. It was the kind of thing a man who has no real hopes for himself will put his whole stock in believing. Or maybe he was just talking to fill the silence.

THEN THE SAD show host, the last show host, did a week's worth of shows about missing girls. They did not ask us back on. They had new families. A whole week's worth of gutted men and women. People I knew better than they knew themselves at that point. They looked into the camera, one from each couple, and said some variation of, Please return our daughter.

Bring back our angel to us. Bring back our light.

Please give us back our daughter.

If you have her, we need her. Please.

Give us our baby back. Bring her home, please.

It is not too late to undo what you've done.

It is not too late to undo what you've done, I tell her Dad.

He's distraught. Won't talk. In his arms, the limp corpse of a young dog.

It has enormous paws. If it had happened a few years later, it might have survived. Might have done some damage to the car even. But, happen as it did, her Dad heard the thing rattling around in the wheel-well before he even realized there was something in the road.

I haven't seen him like this before, really. Not since she vanished. He hears me, but he doesn't like what he's hearing. He looks at me all full of rage then and I mentally prepare for a fight. You have to imagine the first few blows, really feel them, then picture your response. That way, when he lands them, it won't be a shock. You just take it, then respond quickly and powerfully. This is what I've learned.

But this time, we don't fight. He sets the thing on the porch and goes into the garage. He comes out with a hammer and a single nail. He balances the nail on its head, covers its point with his palm, and brings the hammer down just at the top of his wrist. The nail only goes in a little. It barely pokes out the back of his hand. There isn't much blood either. But I heard the wrist break. It was like dropping a bag of rocks. Pieces ground against other pieces, everything moving around. Dust rose and fell. He crumpled up and made some sounds and everything else went back into its place. I went inside and there was Jerry Summers. He looks older with each episode, as if each one takes something particular out of him. And how could it not? He feels everything we feel. He is a man of great capacity, but every person has their limits.

WHAT WAS SHE LIKE?

I DON'T FEEL safe anymore. I haven't since she vanished. And it's only gotten worse. You hear all kinds of sounds at night. I grew up in a place like this. Not far from here actually. Different woods, but woods are woods. As a child, every sound becomes something worse than what it really is. Even if it's something dangerous enough already, it becomes a nightmare in your mind. A tree at the screen becomes a claw. A paw in the grass becomes a bear. And a bear suddenly has an agenda. It knows where you are, and it's coming for you.

So you learn not to listen. You learn not to hear. You turn up the radio. You talk to yourself, late into the night.

I CALLED IN from a payphone near the laundry, but no one answered. I left a message saying that we had been guests on the show, nearly a year ago, and we wanted to come back on. We hadn't heard anything since we'd been on. Nothing had changed except we were more tired now than we'd ever been, thinner. We'd grown farther apart from one another. But the hurt hadn't changed. I wanted to say it was worse, but the truth is that I can't remember a time when I felt any better. There was before, but that's not real anymore. After is all there is.

I CALLED FOR WEEKS and no one answered. It was always a machine. There must have been some glitch on their end. So, I called. And called.

I NEED TO GO by the television station, I told her Dad.

Why?

Because I need to talk to the booker. We need to go back on.

I hadn't wanted to tell him, but it was the only way. He had the car. I don't ride public transportation. I find it depressing.

I don't think that's such a good idea.

Why not?

Because I don't think they'll be able to help us.

Why not? This is what they do! This is how it works, I said.

Maybe, said her Dad. Those shows use people anyway, he said. Here.

He fished a small rock out of his pocket.

It's limestone, he told me.

And I said, so what?

He rubbed it with his thumb like he was cleaning it.

I don't know, he said. I thought you might like it. It's stupid. I'm sorry about the other night, he said.

If you're sorry you'll drive me to the TV station.

So he drove me.

IT WAS THIS KIND of thing for years. He loses his temper. He's an asshole, plain and simple. But he's also naively sweet. He's an idiot is what it is, for the most part. He's this weak little idiot that I could love more than anything in the entire world.

Then she arrived and I loved her that way instead. There was less for him because there had to be. It's the odd thing about a child, you'll sacrifice anything for them, even the person you once loved more than anything else in this world. A person you would have given your own life for, suddenly you'd strike them down to protect something that can't even speak. That just rolls around and makes little sounds and touches your face and fingers and keys indiscriminately.

But so he'd lose his temper and we'd get into it. Then he'd apologize and do something nice for me. Mostly these weren't the right things. The limestone, for example. I can't say what he intended with that. It's a kind of trick. Here is something that looks and sounds like a gift, but that isn't actually a gift. It was a system I learned to game. Reject the first gift and while he's reeling, provide him a new opportunity for redemption.

The tricky part is, I have to really forgive him after. If I don't he knows he's being played. I have to rid myself of anger, fear, resentment. I have to allow myself to love him again.

It isn't hard to do. It's easier than not forgiving. Forgiveness is a strange thing. It accumulates. The more times you've forgiven a person, the more naturally it comes to you, for even the most egregious acts. It's easier than staying mad after it's started to bore you—which it always does eventually. So, knowing as I did that I wasn't going to leave him—it just wasn't going to happen, even if I entertained the notion practically daily—the sanest thing to do was to forgive him.

HER DAD STAYED in the car and smoked through a cracked window. He was nervous, which made me brave. There are few things that give me more pleasure these days than to display the fact that I am stronger than him.

The studio is a few rectangular buildings arranged in a grid. They're guarded by a single security man at the gate. When we were guests, we were escorted. It wasn't a limousine, but one of those classy black cars that looks like a limo but humbler. The driver waved some things and said some things and we got in without a problem.

The security guard stepped out of the booth when he saw me, and I looked back to her Dad sitting there in the car, but only for a second.

Help you?

I'd like to be a guest again, I said. I had to start somewhere. It wasn't what I had planned on saying, but the words sped up and out of my mouth before I could stop them. That made me a little more nervous than I should have been, I think. Feeling suddenly like I was less in control than I thought I would be.

You were a guest? he said.

He reached into the booth and retrieved a clipboard. He looked it over, page after page.

When exactly?

Nearly a year ago, I said. I folded my arms at my chest. We weren't going to be on that list. It was only a couple of sheets. There was no way it had everyone who'd ever been on the show on it. No way.

What was your name again? he asked.

It was about missing children, I said. We lost our daughter.

Oh, he said. I'm sorry.

He looked up. He brought the clipboard down to his side.

I'm sorry, Ma'am.

I nodded. I felt a little more confident then.

You have to be in touch with the production assistant, he said. Laurette, I think. Laurette Conors.

He put the clipboard back and checked another stack of papers.

Yeah, he said, that's her.

I've been calling for weeks, I told him.

I was feeling much better now.

I'm sorry, Ma'am.

I told him not to be sorry. I told him to let me in to talk to this Laurette Conors, or to the sad show host himself.

He nodded and looked to the bushes at his side. He nodded at the bushes then, as if he were talking it over with them.

I'm sorry, Ma'am, but I can't do it.

Can't what? I said.

Can't let you in.

He didn't look up from the bushes.

Are all the men in this world cowards? Is it all hiding and stealing? Is it all sadness and ignored phone calls? Mindless busy work, mindless staring and nodding at bushes? Smoking through a cracked window while your desperate wife pulls at her sweatshirt and faces an enormous man with a gun at his side?

I'm not asking for heroes. I'm asking for people to take responsibility for themselves. I'm asking for at least some of us to have the courage to be up front about what they want, or what they need. When did we learn to hide like this? Who made us this kind of afraid?

You shit, is what I said next. God damn you. If you won't let me in, you'll bring them out here. The moment they see my face, you'll regret this. You'll be fired. You'll be shamed, humiliated. You're a coward, I told him.

He looked at me then like I was his own sick mother.

He went into the booth, tore loose a paper towel, and placed it in my hand.

I let it fall to the blacktop and brought my shoulders back triumphantly.

A coward, I said again.

Finally, I wiped my eyes and cheeks with the back of my right sleeve. I wiped the thin ring of my nostril.

He wasn't going to budge. I thought to turn back, to climb into the car beside her Dad and his unfinished cigarette and tell him, We're coming back tomorrow.

But I stamped the guard's shoe instead. I stamped it hard, with my heel.

I called him a fucker.

He only seemed to get more sad, not angry. It was pathetic. I started to hate him right then and there.

I'll kick you too, I said. I'll start kicking and won't stop until you bring Lauren or whoever and we settle this right here and now.

He limped into the booth and called the police instead. A true blue coward. He probably has a daughter. She probably takes up his gun when he's asleep, or when he's in the bathroom, sitting there, flipping idly through whatever his ex-wife left in the magazine rack, and that daughter probably feels the weight of that gun, the cool metallic sting of it, and she probably tells herself over and over again how powerful her daddy is, how strong, while he applies a folded square of toilet paper to a soggy, stupid, dangling, worthless, dick.

I THOUGHT YOU might come. I'm not going to lie. When the police car turned the corner, I imagined you in the passenger seat, insisting that it was all a huge mistake, that I was who I said I was, that I was a suffering woman who needed help, who needed to be cared for. Not a lunatic attacking security guards for no reason.

But that didn't happen.

Her Dad put out his cigarette. He put his arms around me, led me back to the car, apologizing over and over as he did so.

The security guard let us go. He said something to the cop who had approached me. Who had placed his hand atop his holstered gun. And after they spoke, both men just stood and watched and nodded as her Dad said, I'm sorry for that. She's not well. We're sorry.

I was too angry to speak, so I didn't say anything. Only right before we drove away I put my mouth to the top of the cracked window and called the coward a coward, one last time.

I TOLD HIM I didn't need saving.

The hell you didn't.

Nobody would hear me is all. I wasn't in trouble. They were cowards anyway.

That cop wasn't a coward.

Mick?

No... the cop who... the real cop with a real gun who drove up and got out and would have really arrested you.

I'd love it if he had. To see the look on his face when he found out what he'd done.

We're not going back to that studio.

But—

We're not going back. I won't drive you. If you try to walk there, I'll call them and let them know you're coming. They'll be waiting to put you away. You can count on it.

You're not going to help me?

Not with this.

So I SET THE HOUSE on fire. I'll come clean. No use in hiding it. I told her Dad I was going out to sit on the porch and then I poured gasoline all over the far back corner of the house, by the kitchen. I thought it would catch quickly there, spread more easily. And seeing as it was the corner of the house farthest from the bedroom, I figured he wouldn't die. He would realize what was happening just when the fire got too big to stop, but not so big that he couldn't escape.

I wish big fires moved slowly. Or I wish you could slow them down, see how they leap from one thing to the next. Instead, it swallowed up the slats on the side of the house and spilled onto the roof. It moved like dust across the kitchen floor. It moved relentlessly forward and up and out. I stood back. I watched it work its hardest to take everything.

Eventually I heard him yelling. He yelled my name a few times. Then he came running out of the house, clutching a few of her toys in his arms, and the coffee can we keep our savings in.

He stumbled at the porch and came tumbling onto the lawn. He's an oaf, through and through.

I helped him up and he saw that I wasn't panicking and knew exactly what I'd done.

We had it out there on the lawn. One of the biggest yet. I pulled a branch from the pile he made after mowing that morning and set to hitting him at his sides and face. He didn't swing for a bit, just took the hits, blocking his sensitive parts—eyes, nose, cheeks, etc.—with his forearms. But then he got ahold of me. He set to work on me. I can't say I didn't deserve it. In his eyes, I had tried to kill him. Tried to erase everything we had together.

He hit me in the stomach and I keeled over and he pushed me to the ground. Then he started slapping me. One cheek after the other. He put some grass, some dirt in my mouth. He rubbed it in my eyes and across my forehead, shaming me.

All the while he was saying, What were you thinking? Why didn't you say anything? What are you doing to me? What did I do? What did I ever do?

Not long after that he got down on the grass beside me. I was full of humiliation. He was breathing heavily and I was crying. I turned and put my arms around him, but when he raised the opposite arm to take me up, I flinched. He brought it back down to the earth.

THE FIRE MIGHT have been the best thing I've ever done for him. Think of all he had to do now. All the work. He starting making three trips to the hardware store a day. He piled lumber in the yard, wrapped up in a green tarp. He set to work for real. He gutted the burnt wood that ran the length of the kitchen wall. He had to undo almost everything so he could make it new. It was a tiny blessing. He worked harder than he ever had before.

He was not at a point of forgiving me yet. We didn't speak much. Our nights passed quietly. We were still. I still wasn't sleeping, but after a week of repairing the kitchen, his eyes closed and did not reopen for nearly thirteen hours.

THEN THEY FOUND a child. I cut into the kitchen and took the hammer straight from his hand. He flared up, red-eyed, storming, but I dragged him into the living room and pointed at the television. There sat a family: mother, father, and daughter. The daughter was in blue and white like the Virgin Mary. She sat atop her mother's lap.

He watched for a moment. His anger seemed to leave him like a flock of birds lifting.

What am I doing here? he asked.

They found a girl, I told him.

He nodded, watched the TV.

They're finding girls, I said.

He snatched back the hammer and flung it into the television screen and the screen cracked like a dumb, frozen lake. Not even a spark flew, though the screen did flicker. The sound cut out. Strange light seemed to ooze behind the glass for a moment, then it cut out too.

You've got to stop it with this shit, he told me. We're done with it.

But we weren't done with it. No one was. They were finding girls. There was more to be done. We had been right all along, not to give up hope. There was always a reason to hope, even if just a little. There was proof. Or there had been proof.

He went back to whatever it was he had been doing. It didn't matter anymore. I realized at that exact moment that I would kill him if he got in my way. This was a thought I must have had before, but without realizing it. Or without seeing it so clearly. But then I saw it clear.

Maybe it was what I'd seen, or maybe it was easier to make plans without the TV to distract me. Whatever it was, I was moved to action. I knew what needed to be done, just not exactly how I would go about it. I needed to get in touch with that family, meet that young girl. I needed to know what had happened to her, how she survived. I needed to know how they'd found her. I needed information from the sad show host. I didn't need to go back on the show. Sure, they would have us back on after we'd found her, but that would be an afterthought. If going on the show once had no effect, how could I have thought going on again would fix anything? Where had my head been? Why was it that I could never see things as they are? Why is it that I am always distracted? How did I even survive one day to the next? How did he? We had so little an idea of what was going on around us. We could not do a simple thing like protect her. We could not keep her with us. Everything in our bodies, hearts, and minds had wanted us with her always, but we had let her get away. We'd let her be taken from us. We had no idea how to cherish anything worth cherishing. How to make it last. How to love it and keep it forever. We let the one thing that mattered slip away. And we had been keeping that up. We'd let her slip and keep slipping. But I was going to get her back.

I FELT CLOSE to Mick Something, that we were alike in many ways. I was a woman with a mission. A woman with clarity of vision. These were vigilante cop feelings. I was all the strength I'd ever seen in other people.

I dialed 911 from a payphone down the street. I said I didn't have an emergency, but I needed to talk to the police. They gave me a number to call, but I told them I didn't have any money. Again, I told them it wasn't an emergency. The line went dead. These are our city's emergency services.

I wandered the streets then, full of energy. I saw everything the city had to offer: a row of shops, a neighborhood, some more shops, one house with a bunch of cacti, dead leaves, bushes full of crows, a few creeks along the side of the road, a few overpasses, a hospital that looks like a haunted asylum, men of various ages on skateboards, children in carriages and on bikes, children in parking lots, children in yards, digging at ant beds and thumbing uncracked pecans from the dirt.

There was no way of knowing which house belonged to the family who'd found their daughter. Or whose daughter was found. I didn't even know that much. I knew nothing. After a full day, my energy was waning. I was hot. Thirsty. Call it manic. Call it what you will. The door was open, so I walked in. The bodies were there, so I called 911 again.

I WAS NEVER a suspect, they told me, but I still answered hours of questions. I was in the police station, in a detective's office, for nearly eight hours. I would be called upon again. Maybe to testify. It was hard to say. They would need me to stick around. They had no information regarding my case. They did not know anyone by the name of Mick Something. There were no Micks in the entire department. That got a laugh from some men on the periphery.

The whole thing was a wash. I was worse off than when I started.

Someone had killed two men in their home. Whoever it was, the police told me, had considerable strength. I couldn't have done it because I am weak. I am a small woman. Whoever did this was likely a man. Likely had a reason. Likely didn't like these two men, who were recently married, had a lot of money, and kept to themselves mostly. Our town is not a great place to live for anyone, especially anyone who is particularly happy. Our town is filled with people who want to reach in and take your happiness from you. They want to stamp it out with their shitty heel.

The police asked me about the bruises, and I told them I gave them to myself—which is partly true. No one thinks to say that to a police officer. People always blame the house. They say it was an accident. But if a cop is asking, he already knows it wasn't an accident. They can just see it. They sense it. They can smell it on you. So I told him I did it to myself. I talked about the different ways I had done it: a grocery bag full of apples, dropping myself, open mouth first, onto the counter edge, running into the stairs, rolling myself down them. I said I was working out some feelings about my missing daughter. They asked how long she had been missing. I tried to tell them the whole story, all over again. Only this time, it felt different.

They asked what she looked like. I couldn't remember.

They asked how old, and I said, about two and a half?

They asked if she was my daughter by birth, or if she was adopted. Birth, I told them.

When did you give birth, then?

About... two and a half years ago, I told them.

Her Dad showed up then.

I was cold and he put his arms around me.

He talked to the police for only a little while. They wanted to take him into a room without me, but I didn't want him to go. It was not an easy day for me. I was not comfortable or safe. He had on two shirts and he put one on me, an orange flannel, so that he could sort of be with me and I could be a little warmer, but then he left me and went into an office with an officer.

They talked for a while and then we left.

He looked good. His neck and wrists were burned by the sun. His beard was trimmed, practically tame. His other shirt was a tight-fitting wife-beater, one that had only weeks ago hung from him like a dishrag on a line. His hands, his arms were steady. He watched the road, and every so often he took one hand off the wheel and rested his arm in his lap. He looked healthy. Like he might have when we met, if he hadn't been so awful then.

When we got home, we sat on the couch together, in front of the broken television.

We didn't say anything for a long time, and then her Dad said, Our hero, Mick Something, was nearly crushed by the ten tons of steel pouring from the back of the 18-wheeler as he pursued it along the coastal highway.

Any other fool, I added, might have seen the spill as a tragic accident. But the moment Mick Something noticed how the steel had been stacked—loosely, its scarred edge pointing out from the back— he knew something foul was afoot.

The steel came loose, as if it were born to do so, and came clattering toward our hero in his rusted-out jalopy.

It looked like lights-out for Mick, he had nearly bitten the hard steel when a runaway truck ramp appeared at the left. He jerked the wheel, his tires spinning in the dirt and loose gravel, and he began to steadily climb the ramp.

The steel covered the highway, screeching and clanging and screaming like a pack of wild birds. The 18-wheeler disappeared over the horizon.

Mick slammed the brakes. Nothing. He reached for the emergency break, but the lever came off in his hand. The car sped toward the end of the ramp, where it plateaued only briefly before dropping back down, several hundred feet, to the rock bed below.

It looked like curtains for Mick.

He'd really outdone himself this time.

The car was slowing down, but not fast enough.

Mick launched.

He sailed through the air, turning, the wheels spinning.

His hair blew gracefully in the breeze.

The steel clattered on behind him.

He rose for only a few seconds before he began to fall.

He fell and fell, for what felt like forever.

WE SLEPT ON the couch together that night, her Dad and I. Or, truthfully, he slept with his arms around me and I stared for hours at the broken television. I looked out the window too, but I could only see a reflection of myself.

There is nothing worse than dark windows in a still house at night. Nothing worse than your own reflection where the rest of the world should be.

I pinched his nose and after a few seconds he woke with a start. He pushed himself up and off the couch, swatting at his nostrils. He blew out a few times, as if bugs had made their way into the cavities.

What happened? I asked.

He looked around. He was still waking up, realizing where he was.

Felt like I stopped breathing, he said.

Oh?

Did I? Did you hear me stop?

I shook my head. I hadn't noticed anything, just him leaping up and flailing, I told him.

IN THE MORNING, we had breakfast. I cooked like a champion. I cooked like a sane woman. A sane human being. I felt sane. I'd watched him sleep, and he looks as lovely as a duckling when he's asleep. He still looks like him, I mean. He's not any more handsome than he is during the daytime. But he looks soft and tender, looks like something you'd want to hold to your breast and whisper to. Not like a baby, but like a kitten. Not a human thing, really.

He was this beautiful non-human thing, and I made him breakfast.

I hadn't done it for something like two years. Even when I was making breakfast before, I was thinking only of her. I can't remember if I excluded him purposefully, or if the thought that I was doing so occurred to me later, occurred to me only recently, now that I've the time to wonder about that kind of thing.

OTHER LETTERS TO MICK SOMETHING

Dear Mr. Mick Something,

Today we made a wet kind of thing out of flour and water and salt. When you touched it, it got hard. When you let your hand just sit there, it slid through your fingers. We made a mess and that was part of it. Everybody had a good time, even the ones who don't always have a good time. I always have a good time because I'm a good student at school and I like to be.

Thank you.

DEAR MICK SOMETHING,

Thank you for your talk today in school. I learned that we should be careful and watch out for our friends and for ourselves. Thank you for the talk and for telling us the Five Things to Always Be on the Lookout For. I will be on the Lookout For them. I promise.

Sincerely.

DEAR MICK SOMETHING,

You won't get away with it, because I'm onto you.

WHILE HE REPAIRED the house my hair went white and I became attractive to other men. One man came up to the back fence. I was wandering the border of our yard. We have no fences on either the left or right side of us, only one in the back, which separates our lawn from that which belongs to the State. The State's lawn goes on for miles, and that is where the new man came from, some great distance away. We tried to make a child without saying anything. Right there on the lawn of the State. Today I can tell you we were not successful, but for months this was something I saw as more than possible, possibly inevitable. I was long without any real sense of what could happen next, so I imagined something might happen that would pull me out of all of this stillness. I dreaded it as much as I hoped for it.

I was wandering a lot at the time, escaping the ongoing noise of her Dad's repairs, so he thought little of it when I began to leave the house, almost daily, to retreat to the lawn of the State. Eventually, always, the other man came. We were without ceremony, without words. It was as cold as any exchange could ever be, but still a perfect, clean encounter. There was a beginning, middle, and end. We departed without any unpleasant passings. Once, during the middle part, I whispered something to him. He put his finger to my lips and we continued on to the end. Another time, he said something like you are beautiful into my hair, just behind my ear. He was very quiet. They were hardly even words. In all honesty, it could have been the mud shifting beneath us. It was entirely perfect.

HER DAD CHANGED the house. He built the kitchen out, added a turn to its center. The house had too many angles now, and I kept bumping into things. He began to relax. He drank beers and slept during the day. I caught him on the porch one afternoon, gazing at a long green caterpillar on his finger. It moved slowly from the tip back to his hand when he turned it. He was even smiling underneath the nod he gave me. It was nearly sunset. It was an ideal scene. I could feel that the other man was somewhere out there, steadily approaching our back fence while her Dad just sat there watching an insect grapple for footing.

We were in a new place. He was someone completely different. I walked past him and the caterpillar, on to the gate. The other man did not come, so I circled out there until the sun was completely gone. Her Dad yelled something to me, but I could not hear it. It was something about the wind. Something about a storm. He worries.

WHAT WAS SHE LIKE?
krrrrraaaackkkkkk

What was our daughter like?
boomhhhhh

WE HAD ANOTHER bad night together. A particularly bad one. The kind of bad I couldn't ignore. I couldn't let it sit. Some kinds of bad can't be undone.

THE PLANKS WERE not held down. There were holes where the nails should be. Tiny, rusted holes. So the planks came loose with little effort. Under the porch, it's just dirt and a few bits of trash drawn there by the wind. I didn't know the kind of work I had ahead of me. I'm not a digger. I worked the earth for nearly an hour and had little more than a ditch. In a quilt, he seemed enormous. I just kept digging while the wind tossed the edges of the quilt around.

Eventually, the hole was nearly big enough. Then I hit something. Something firm but soft and smooth, like a stone at the bottom of a lake. I already knew what it was without looking, but I brushed the dirt aside with my palms and fingers all the same. She was mostly bone, wrapped in a thin layer of matted hair. It was short. He must have cut it. My second thought was that it wasn't her. That there was no reason to believe it was her. That maybe it felt like her because some part of me wanted it to be her. Some part of me just wanted it all over and to know and to be done with it. That part of me was staring at the hair and trying to see it as an animal's, trying to take the mud-caked mess into it as its natural color. That part of me was seeing a dead coyote and an old t-shirt and hearing the wind chimes tremble and maybe even a car approaching.

HER BONES MADE only a small pile, gathered together. I had a sense of where some of them went, but not all. I would like to think I knew my daughter so well that I could identify each and every part of her. Any mother would like to think that probably. But it isn't true. Her Dad might have pretended to know. He might have worked this into that, gummed one end and stuck it to the crook of another, but he was gone.

I stopped worrying about what went where and I gathered them together in a little bundle I could get my arms around and wrapped them up in a t-shirt. They had a musty smell, nothing too unsettling. They smelled like a grandparent or an old closet.

I'm worried this is all making me sound a little crazy. I'm just trying to tell you what happened, not why. Why has nothing to do with what, really. Not when it comes to this kind of thing. The why is ongoing and unsettled—always. And if anyone ever tries to tell you different, run.

How could you kill a man who loved you? A man you claimed to
have loved as well?

I know now that what I did was right, but I did not know it at
the time. I felt it had to be done and I did it, only to discover I had
done the right thing. The hours he spent on the porch, his constant
movement about the house. He knew all along that she was there. He
was hiding it. The only imaginable reason for doing so is that he was
the one who had put her there.

What proof do you have?

The proof of the feeling and its confirmation. I knew I had to kill
him, though I did not know why. I knew I had to bury him beneath the
porch, keep him nearby, and again without a clear reason. I knew the
truth before I understood it. I knew the truth before it was confirmed
as such.

Were you aware that it is more often the case than not that parents are
involved in the disappearance of a child? Parents or loved ones? It is
almost always someone close?

I did not choose to believe it, but I was told as much by the sad
show host at the end of the week dedicated to missing children.

Were you offended by the timing of the presentation of that information?

I was offended by every aspect of the presentation of that information. The sad show host was someone I did not miss after the breaking of the television.

Have you any remaining desire to appear on his show? To present your child? To present your story?

Every day I am struck with the desire to tell everyone all the details of my story. I am rarely without that feeling.

To what end?

At first, I wanted nothing more than to find my child. The more people who knew about her, the more eyes we had on the world. I was without the ability to censor myself. Each time I told someone new, I felt we were moving forward in her pursuit. I did not ever want to be without that feeling.

And now?

I do not want these feelings to die with me.

Do you think about death often? Do you have an idea of how it might happen?

Yes.

How do you think it will happen?

I think I will vanish. I will disappear without reappearing.

Where will you go?

Nowhere. I will just be gone.

What makes you feel that way?

I simply do. I can imagine it more clearly than anything I have imagined before. It is what will happen.

Why?

That part doesn't matter.

What is your daughter like?

She is a tender, whispering sack of bones.

.

SHE WAS A SILENT kind of beautiful. The fabric of the shirt that held her smoothed the edges of the more jagged bones. I ran my finger along her little curves and watched the windows as the night moved past them. Every now and then, the coyotes would gather outside and make those dreadful sounds. It was frightening without her Dad there and his shovel. But it was nothing I couldn't handle. She was safe with me, and I knew coyotes weren't something I needed to be afraid of. It's just the sounds they make. The way they become more than coyotes. Like one of those nightmares where you know you're dreaming but you can't wake yourself up. You just have to sit there and be afraid and let whatever it is wash over you.

In my nightmares, the terror never recedes. It is always building up around me, toward me, while I wait. If I could learn to not be afraid of what I can't prevent, then I could sleep a little more soundly, maybe. Did I mention I've been sleeping again? Not for more than a few moments at a time, but sleeping nonetheless. We sleep on the couch together, she and I. It's pleasant enough to drift off every now and again.

I am not so deranged that I don't notice how different this creature is than the one that came before. I am not so deranged that I don't know she is, in fact, not a creature at all. I still love her. She is still the light of my life. It's just a different quality of light. I can hold the whole of her in my arms, and I will be forever able to. Can you imagine? Even when I held her as an infant, some part of me sensed the shifts taking place right there in my arms. She was always growing. Stretching out and getting heavier. I would look away for only a moment, and she'd be up an inch, snatching something off the counter or pulling something sharp from a drawer. That will never be the case again. She will forever and always be this perfect little armful.

I marvel at this perfect animal armful and wonder how I could have ever doubted her existence. There was a time when I became so overwhelmed with missing her that I tried to erase her. My mind tried to reject what was killing it, the notion that she was out there somewhere and that I could not help her. Could not have her.

Now I have her again. Now she is here with me. And all of my love comes rushing up and through me and I feel like a perfect creature again. I feel like a mother. When I lift the shirt that holds her together the bones click and rustle against one another like a bucketful of shells. I consider all the places I could take her: the beach, the grocery, the park, another state, another country. I could carry her along with me while I travel the world. I'm excited. My hands shake when I do regular things like tear loose a square of toilet paper or try to pour the milk.

I am no longer concerned with appearing strong for her. I feel strong, but I will melt in front of her, on top of her, into her. I collapse with regularity now. I hit the floor like an old branch. I crawl and weep like a child. She sits and sees it all. I show her what a feeling is. I become sadness. I become anger. I become that numb kind of quiet. I hum alongside her on the couch for hours. She doesn't complain. She can't, I know that. I am not delusional. But objects have an air of judgment about them all their own. The rocks feel our feet. The trees smell us in the yard. The stairs hear our footfalls, our farts, when we yell and scream at one another. Beds breathe in our tenderness. And in this measured way, my daughter came to know me.

ACKNOWLEDGMENTS

Thanks to my reader, editor, and life coach: Andi Winnette. Thanks
to Mauro Cardenas, Daniel Levin Becker, Alice Kim, Reese Kwon,
Vauhini Vara, and Esmé Wang for talking this through with me. Thanks
to J.A. Tyler. Thanks to Adam Robinson. Thanks to Aimee Bender,
Vanessa Place, Andrew Wessels, Teresa Carmody, and everyone at Les
Figues who work so hard.

Thanks to Julie, Miles, Katie, and Adam.

ABOUT THE AUTHOR

Colin Winnette is the author of several books, including *Fondly*, listed among Salon's "best books of 2013." He is an associate editor for *PANK*. Links to his stories, poems, and interviews with writers he admires can be found at colinwinnette.net. He lives in San Francisco.